Esther,

What a pleasure & honor it has been working with you. I wish you the very best in your new adventure!! You're work and the foundation you have laid for the PACT program will live on... but we will miss you!

♡ Nancy
Jan 2019

Also by JoAnne Dodgson

Unleashing Love
Gifts of the Grandmother

SPIRIT OF CHOCOLATE

*A Woman's Journey to the Rainforest
in Search of Her Dreams*

JoAnne Dodgson

BALBOA
PRESS

A DIVISION OF HAY HOUSE

This is a work of fiction. All of the characters, names, incidents, organizations, and dialogue
in this novel are either the products of the author's imagination or are used fictitiously.

Cover art by JoAnne Dodgson; digital colorization by Angela Werneke

Balboa Press books may be ordered through booksellers or by contacting:

Balboa Press
A Division of Hay House
1663 Liberty Drive
Bloomington, IN 47403
www.balboapress.com
1 (877) 407-4847

Because of the dynamic nature of the Internet, any web addresses or links contained in
this book may have changed since publication and may no longer be valid. The views
expressed in this work are solely those of the author and do not necessarily reflect the
views of the publisher, and the publisher hereby disclaims any responsibility for them.

The author of this book does not dispense medical advice or prescribe the use of any
technique as a form of treatment for physical, emotional, or medical problems without the
advice of a physician, either directly or indirectly. The intent of the author is only to offer
information of a general nature to help you in your quest for emotional and spiritual well-
being. In the event you use any of the information in this book for yourself, which is your
constitutional right, the author and the publisher assume no responsibility for your actions.

Any people depicted in stock imagery provided by Thinkstock are models,
and such images are being used for illustrative purposes only.
Certain stock imagery © Thinkstock.

Print information available on the last page.

ISBN: 978-1-5043-9189-4 (sc)
ISBN: 978-1-5043-9191-7 (hc)
ISBN: 978-1-5043-9190-0 (e)

Library of Congress Control Number: 2017917620

Balboa Press rev. date: 11/29/2017

Contents

for our Mother Earth and all the generations to come

Preface

Dear Reader,

Spirit of Chocolate was inspired over ten years ago. Spending afternoons in a chocolate shop, writing stories and sipping spicy elixirs, ignited my passion for the heart-opening medicines of cacao (ka-KOW). I was compelled to learn more about the ancient traditions surrounding this sacred food. I was enchanted by the cacao tree and the seeds from which chocolate is made.

For years, the vision for this book has been held close in my heart, embraced by friends, and honored in ceremonial ways. The story has been simmering, shifting, deepening over time, and finally is ready to be shared.

Spirit of Chocolate weaves together many passions in my life—my love for stories, for our Mother Earth, for ancestral traditions, for dreaming new dreams, and for personal healing that transforms our lives and our world.

I invite you to join me in this journey through the rainforest. Flourish in the beauty of the tree frogs, the mystery of the jaguar, the passion of Thea's spiritual quest, the wisdom of the Old Woman, and the gifts shared so generously by Ka`Kao.

May *Spirit of Chocolate* carry you home to your heart and to the awakening of harmony in your life and on our earth.

Manaole U Manaole,
From my heart to the heart of the Mother Earth to your heart,

JoAnne

Introduction

The story of chocolate begins in the rainforest with a tree who lives in the shade beneath the jungle canopy. Cacao (ka-KOW) tree is quite extraordinary, simply like no other. She's a magical, mystical tree.

Symbolically in ancient art and stories, cacao represents nourishment, life potentials, natural cycles, connectedness, and fertility. Cacao is associated with the Great Mystery, with the unseen and magical realms. In indigenous cultures in Central and South America, the cacao tree is considered the World Tree, the Tree of Life, the Tree at the Center of the Universe. Cacao is life that feeds life that feeds life.

Her roots: Cacao's homeland is the rainforest. In the wild, she flourishes in the rainy, hot, and humid lands twenty degrees north and twenty degrees south of the equator. Cacao tree depends on taller trees to provide shade. These protective trees, called mother trees, include the banana, coconut palm, and lemon.

In the shaded land beneath the jungle canopy, the tender vine-like cacao tree thrives.

Her flowers: Cacao's flowers are quite unique. They don't only grow on the ends of the branches, nor do the flowers bloom just seasonally. The tiny pink and white flowers spiral around the tree trunk and along the branches. The flowers bud and blossom throughout the year. Cacao blossoms have no scent, at least to our human noses.

Midges, little flying insects, seek out the pollen inside the cacao blossoms. As the midges fly among the trees, the cacao pollen carried on the midges' bodies gets transferred from flower to flower. Once pollinated, the flowers transform into fruits.

Her pods: Cacao's unusual fruit pods also hint at the magic of this tree. The fruit pods are thick-skinned, deeply ribbed, oval bulbs, some weighing over one pound. Cacao pods are a unique rainbow of colors—red, green, yellow, violet, brown, and orange—depending on the particular tree species and ripeness of the fruits. Cacao pods spiral around the trunk and hang from all parts of the branches, just as the flowers do.

Cacao's pods don't drop to the ground when the fruit is ripe. Each pod is filled with a succulent, creamy pulp that draws monkeys, bats, and parrots for a delectable feast. When the fruit pulp is eaten, the seeds inside the pod may be inadvertently consumed or dropped to the ground. The animals and birds naturally disperse the pods and seeds, planting the next generation of cacao trees.

Her seeds: Cacao seeds are the part of the tree used to make chocolate. Cacao seeds are highly nutritious and have unique chemical compounds that provide energy for the human body, generate feelings of well-being, and evoke altered states of consciousness. Ancient peoples knew this, and contemporary science bears this out.

In traditional ways of preparing cacao, the seeds are gathered from the pods, fermented with the pulp, and dried in the sun. The seeds are then roasted, winnowed, and ground into a velvety paste. Cacao elixirs, a warm beverage, are made by mixing the cacao paste with water and spices such as cinnamon, chili, and vanilla bean. In ancient and contemporary cultures, cacao elixirs are enjoyed for daily nourishment and consumed for ceremonial purposes.

Her magic: In Mayan traditions, the spirit of cacao has been described as the water that runs through the heart. Cacao has been given the name Theobroma, food of the gods.

When eating and drinking cacao, we are touching, tasting, embodying, and sharing the seed of the Tree of Life. Cacao provides nourishment for body, mind, heart, and spirit. Cacao is sacred medicine.

The ancient ways of Ka Ta See are woven into *Spirit of Chocolate*. Ka Ta See is a tribal way of life that has been lived and protected for tens of thousands of years. Chea and Domano Hetaka, elders and lineage-carriers of Ka Ta See, made their way from Peru to North America in the 1970s. The elders were on a quest to find a student with whom they would share their traditional medicine ways.

The elders understood the world was spinning out of balance, that people were buried in stress, addictions, judgments, and fears. Following the prophecies of their people, the elders shared their way of life to assist humanity's awakening. The elders trusted in our ability to wake up, to remember the beauty and truths of our humanness, to live in heart-centered ways and create a heart-centered world.

When translating their ways to English language, the elders chose the word "Song" to describe each individual's genuine beingness, the true self, the knowing of who and what you really are. Everyone has a Song—every human, every tree, every rock, every grain of sand. All the Songs are connected in the vast web of life on earth and far beyond. Remembering your Song, living and being your Song, is a central aspect of the Ka Ta See ways.

The Hetakas found their student, Kay Cordell Whitaker, who then apprenticed with the elders for thirteen years. I have had the privilege of apprenticing with Kay to learn and live the ways of the *kala keh nah seh*—medicine storyteller, weaver of webs of balance, healer, teacher, and ceremonial guide.

Spirit of Chocolate is shared with deep respect for the elders who gave us the gifts of their teachings to awaken our hearts and weave balance on our earth.

Spirit of Chocolate is my offering of gratitude for the medicines of cacao, the magic of the rainforest, and for dreaming new dreams for a loving, harmonious world.

References

Coe, Sophia D., and Michael D. Coe. *The True History of Chocolate*. London: Thames & Hudson, 1996, 2007.

Dreiss, Meredith L., and Sharon Edgar Greenhill. *Chocolate: Pathway to the Gods*. Tucson: University of Arizona Press, 2008.

McNeil, Cameron L. (ed.) *Chocolate in Mesoamerica: A Cultural History of Cacao*. Gainesville: University of Florida Press, 2006.

Whitaker, Kay C. *The Reluctant Shaman: A Woman's First Encounters with the Unseen Spirits of the Earth*. New York: HarperCollins, 1991.

Prelude

When tree frogs sing
They fill the rainforest
With their colorful voices
With the very breath of life

The trees breathe this in
Soaking up the sharing
Then the trees breathe out
Sending waves of the breath of life
Rippling through the rainforest and far beyond

So when tree frogs sing
They feed the rainforest
And the breath of the rainforest
Feeds the Mother Earth
Filling the world with harmony
Weaving the web of life with love

Something's Missing

I used every ounce of strength I had to push the raft upstream. River currents tugged against my legs. Gusts of wind blew me sideways. Sheets of rain blurred my vision. The thundering roar of the downpour was the only sound I could hear.

My body ached with sheer exhaustion. The fear of snakes and jaguars made my stomach clench. I was terrified of getting dragged under by the turbulent waters. I stopped to catch my breath, trying to muster up enough courage to take another step.

This was not at all what I had planned. This was supposed to be the adventure of a lifetime. A chance to start over. I'd left everyone and everything behind because something was missing. I thought I'd find it out here in the exotic lands of the rainforest, far away from home in unfamiliar terrain.

I pushed against the river currents, trying to recall what I'd been so certain I would find. Maybe happiness? Love? A sense of belonging? But all I had to show for my sacrifice and struggle was a long list of failures and a bunch of lost dreams.

I pulled the raft onto the riverbank and collapsed on the ground. The wet leaves offered a comforting softness. I couldn't hold back my grief. I didn't even try to stop the flood of tears. There was nobody there to hide from.

As the sky blazed red with the setting sun, my remaining hopes became quite singular. I simply wanted to fade away, riding the waves of disappointment into everlasting sleep.

Tree of Life

Ka'Kao Tree lived in the center of the rainforest. She was a magical tree, a mystical tree. She knew the languages of those who walked on the land, swam in the waters, rooted in the soil, and soared on wings. She listened to the rocks and the winds, the rivers and the rain. She lived in rhythm with the cycles of the sun and the moon, with the galaxy and all that's beyond. She nourished and cherished the vast web of life. The love she shared had no bounds.

Ka`Kao Tree watched over the changes on the earth. For many generations, the world had been spinning out of balance. Waters were poisoned. Animals and plants weren't allowed to naturally grow. People were at war against themselves and each other. The rainforest was being cut down.

Ka`Kao understood this path of destruction could continue. Or the tide could be turned and harmony restored. It was up to the people of the earth to choose.

The sign Ka`Kao had been waiting for had finally come. On this night, unlike any other night that had ever been, the tree frogs did not sing.

3

Keeper of the Fire

Ka`Kao Tree called to the winds to blow blossoms
from her branches and carry them all the way to the
Old Woman by the River, the Keeper of the Fire.

Bright golden sparks lit up the night as the shower of ka`kao blossoms fell into the flames. The Old Woman listened to the messages sent to her on the winds. The tree frogs were not singing.

The Old Woman rustled through her baskets and found the pouch of tree resin. She selected one amber nugget and held it out in the palm of her hand. Her heart filled with the promise she'd made long ago with Ka`Kao. When the sign from the tree frogs indicated it was time, the Old Woman and Ka`Kao Tree would help the people of the earth reclaim what had been lost and forgotten. Even if one person fell in love with life again, a river of change would begin to flow. Even if just one person chose to live in heart-centered ways, a powerful momentum would be set in motion for creating a heart-centered world.

The Old Woman dropped the amber nugget onto a smoldering coal. A sweet fragrance rose into the air, beckoning the Old Woman's friend to join her by the fire. With sleek elegance and grace, Jaguar leapt out of the darkness and into the glow of the firelight.

The Old Woman and the wildcat warmly greeted each other and sat together by the fire.

The Old Woman pushed aside a heavy flat rock set in the ground near her feet. With her bare hands, she dug deeper into the soil. She uncovered the clay bowl that had been buried for safekeeping countless generations before. With tenderness and care, she lifted the ancient vessel out of the ground. She brushed away clumps of dirt to reveal the designs carved on the bowl. She traced her fingers along the symbols that described the turning of the times on the earth.

Gazing into the fire, the Old Woman told Jaguar the stories he'd heard her share many times before. About the people of the earth forgetting who they really are. About the world spinning out of balance. About the sign from the tree frogs, the silence of their songs. About the seeds holding new dreams for a heart-centered world.

The Old Woman pried open the sealed lid of the ancient clay bowl. She gently unfolded delicate layers of faded tapestry and lifted up the crystal that had been wrapped inside. She cradled the gemstone in her hands and reached out to show Jaguar. The crystal sparkled and glowed, catching the flickering light of the fire. The wildcat leaned in closer to examine the sacred stone.

The Old Woman held in her mind's eye a picture of Ka`Kao Tree in the center of the rainforest. Jaguar immediately understood the Old Woman's request. With his powerful jaws, he plucked the crystal from the Old Woman's outstretched hands. He leapt over the fire and disappeared into the dark jungle night.

4

Come out of Hiding

I opened my eyes, jolted out of my dreamless sleep. Dazed and disoriented, I looked around trying to figure out where I was. I wasn't sure how long I'd been asleep—maybe hours, maybe minutes—but the darkness of nighttime had come. I strained to push myself up, groaning about the pain that flooded through my body. My heart sank when I saw my raft stranded on the riverbank. I was lost and alone, a long way from home. I wished I'd never woken up.

The smell of something burning caught my attention. A shiver of hope ran up my spine. Smoke meant there was fire. And fire meant there were people. And those people were my only hope for getting help.

The rush of these thoughts gave me enough strength to get on my feet. I followed the smoky scent up the riverbank, pushing my way through the branches, slipping and sliding through the mud.

Finally, I came upon the source of the smoke. There was a pile of glowing coals in a forest clearing. I hid behind the bushes and peeked through the tangle of vines. Time seemed to slow as I pieced together the incomprehensible sight.

An old woman. A jaguar. Together by the fire. Out here in the middle of nowhere.

None of this made any sense. I crouched lower behind the vines, barely daring to breathe. I saw the old woman hand the wildcat something that sparkled in the firelight. The jaguar grabbed the shiny object with his ferocious jaws and darted off into the rainforest.

My heart pounded. The jaguar was on the loose. He could easily hunt me down.

"What are you hiding from?" The voice startled me. The old woman was in the clearing, standing nearby, just on the other side of the vines. So peaceful and steady, she seemed rooted in the earth. Her eyes glistened like stars.

Looking directly at me, she held up a bowl that was cradled in the palms of her hands. The unwavering kindness in the old woman's eyes reached past my fears, touching me. She set the bowl on the ground just out of my reach. Then she turned and walked back to the fire.

I was starved for human companionship. I yearned to feel safe. This drove me to come out of my hiding place.

5

Time for Remembering

On high alert for any signs of danger, I stepped out from behind the tangle of vines. I knelt down and picked up the bowl the old woman had placed on the ground. The bowl was heavy and filled to the brim with a thick liquid. It smelled delicious, but I was hesitant to take a drink. I looked suspiciously at the old woman. She seemed completely unconcerned about me as she tended to the fire.

The alluring fragrance rising out of the bowl reminded me of chocolate delicacies baking in a warm, cozy kitchen. I couldn't resist and took a sip. Intrigued by the flavor, I drank more of the spicy, chocolatey brew. The tension in my body began melting away. I slowly inched closer to the fire. Eventually I sat down on a tree stump beside the old woman. I stared into the flames, not sure what else to do.

"Thank you," I whispered, glancing sideways at the old woman. She seemed perfectly content as she focused on the fire. She stirred the glowing embers with a gnarled tree branch and dropped twigs and bark into the flames.

"My name is Thea," I said, trying to make conversation. I wondered what she thought of me, showing up out of the blue. I hoped a polite introduction would make up for the intrusion.

The old woman smiled softly. She tossed a handful of leaves and berries onto a stone nestled in a bed of hot coals. She ground crunchy dried seeds between two heavy rocks, creating a thick, dark paste. She poured the velvety paste into a clay cooking pot and sprinkled in a few pinches of the fire-roasted spices.

Moving with quiet deliberation, the old woman was entirely engaged with her tasks. Her pure focus was unnerving. The silence between us was uncomfortable.

"I'm lost," I told the old woman. My words were swallowed up by the endless darkness of the jungle night.

The old woman kept stirring the concoction brewing over the fire. I wondered if she'd heard me. Maybe she didn't understand. I felt the panic rising in my throat.

"I'm lost," I pleaded, on the verge of tears, afraid my cry for help might never be heard.

The old woman finally turned and looked at me.

"Feeling lost means something has been forgotten," she said. "It's time for remembering."

I frowned, puzzled by her words.

"Go to the center of the rainforest," the old woman said. "There's someone there waiting for you."

I stood up abruptly, scared and confused. The bowl slipped out of my hands and landed with a thud.

"Go now," the old woman said, her voice more insistent. She tossed an armful of sticks onto the fire, which roared to life with sky-reaching flames.

Startled, I stumbled backward. I looked frantically at the blazing fire, the spilled drink, the old woman. I turned away and ran into the dark jungle night.

6

To the Center of the Rainforest

I ran as fast as I could, stumbling through the darkness, desperate to get far away from the old woman. I tripped over rocks and slipped in the mud.

Angrily, I swatted at the invisible swarms of buzzing, biting insects. Consumed by thoughts of the jaguar, I feared every step could be my last.

When daylight filtered through the rainforest canopy, I was surprised I had survived the long, lonely night. Exhausted, I found shelter beneath the branches of a tree. Thunder drummed overhead as torrential rains fell. I dropped into a heavy sleep.

In the steamy afternoon heat, I woke up into a vibrant world teeming with life. Despite the angst of my situation, I was struck by the beauty of my surroundings. The flowers were a rainbow of vivid blues, yellows, and reds. Towering trees and dense vines created a canopy high overhead. Bright shafts of sunlight trickled through the leaves. A loud clamor of unusual sounds echoed through the thick, humid air.

The tree that provided me shelter was unlike any other tree I'd ever seen. Clusters of tiny blossoms spiraled around the trunk and along the spindly branches. There was a surprising array of fruit pods of diverse colors, sizes, and shapes.

As I walked around the tree, admiring the quirky beauty, a brilliant flash of emerald green caught my attention. A little red-eyed tree frog was hopping from leaf to leaf. He landed on a golden pod, his sticky-toed orange feet gripping the wrinkled shell.

I noticed the golden pod had been chewed open. Curious, I leaned in to have a closer look. Drawn by the sweet smell, I reached inside the pod and scooped up a bit of fruity pulp. I tried a little bite. It tasted refreshing and delicious.

"You've come a long way, Thea." The voice drifted through the branches and rustled the leaves.

Bewildered, I stared at the tree. "How do you know me?" I asked. My mind raced with confusion and fear.

"My name is Ka`Kao," she said. "We're happy you're here." Gentle waves of kindness rippled through the tree, washing over me. The distress of my journey suddenly welled up and poured out. I told Ka`Kao about the horrible storm and how I got stranded on the riverbank. I described every detail of the scary encounter with the old woman and the jaguar. I went on and on about the other hardships I'd faced. Ka`Kao didn't say a word, but I sensed she was listening.

"This was meant to be a fantastic new beginning," I explained. "I left everyone and everything behind." I told her about the freedom I craved, the happiness and love I'd hoped to find.

"But it's been a disaster," I said, stating the obvious, embarrassed by how miserably I'd failed. "I'm completely lost." My voice wavered as I choked back my tears. "I don't know where I am. I don't know which way to go. I don't know what I should do."

"You found your way here," said Ka`Kao, "just as the Old Woman by the River trusted you could."

I stared wide-eyed at the tree. This is who the old woman had sent me off to meet?

"There's something I want to show you," Ka`Kao said. "First, get some rest. Have something to eat."

Many unanswered questions lingered in the air. Yet Ka`Kao's warm welcoming convinced me to stay, at least for awhile anyway. I harvested more fruit from the pods of the tree. After finishing my feast, I stretched out near Ka`Kao's roots.

The next thing I knew I woke up in the pitch-blackness of the night. I held my breath, trying to see into the darkness, listening for any signs of danger. Howler monkeys howled. Owls hooted. Cicadas chirped. Lightning bugs flickered bright flashes of light.

When the sun finally rose, I realized something was missing. I could see tiny, colorful frogs crawling up the tree trunk, hopping from leaf to leaf, and lining up along the branches. The songs of the tree frogs usually filled the rainforest night. But I hadn't heard a single peep.

"Why aren't the tree frogs singing?" I asked.

"The silence of the tree frogs is a sign that our world is spinning out of balance. The fibers in the web of life are tattered and torn," Ka`Kao explained. "The tree frogs are calling to the people of the earth to bring the harmony back."

I looked around at the gathering of the red-eyed tree frogs. They were small and delicate, yet their call to the people of the earth was quite bold.

"How can we bring the harmony back?" I asked

Ka`Kao, overwhelmed by the enormity of the task. "The silence of the tree frogs. The world spinning out of balance. This is all much bigger than me," I muttered, sinking into a familiar pit of despair. "I have more than enough problems of my own," I said, trying to defend myself. Who I was fighting against I really didn't know.

"You can bring the harmony back," Ka`Kao said brightly. "Anyone can. Everyone can. In the everyday moments of everyday life."

"But I'm lost," I argued, not sure she understood my dire circumstances.

"It's time for remembering," said Ka`Kao.

I slumped to the ground with a heavy sigh. The old woman by the river had told me this too. I shut my eyes, trying hard to listen.

"It's time to remember what lives in your heart," Ka`Kao said. "This is where freedom and love have their roots. This is how happiness and harmony come alive."

I glanced at the tree, feeling a glimmer of hope.

"What you are searching for," said Ka`Kao, "is ready and waiting to be found."

7

Dream a New Dream

Following Ka'Kao's instructions, I dug a hole in the ground near her roots. Using stones and sticks, I scraped aside layers of wet leaves, faded blossoms, and crumpled pods. I knelt on the ground, widening and deepening the hole with my bare hands. The soil felt rich and smelled full of life. After I lined the bottom of the hole with broad, waxy leaves, I looked to Ka`Kao, wondering what to do next.

"Harvest one of the pods," she said. "Find the seeds inside." I circled around Ka`Kao Tree, trying to decide which fruit pod to choose. An emerald frog hopped up and down on a brown pod. Maybe I was imagining things, but I felt the red-eyed tree frog was helping me choose just the right one.

I twisted and turned the stem of the pod until it broke away from the branch. With a sharp-edged rock, I cut through the thick brown hull. Inside the pod, rows of almond-shaped seeds were buried in the soft, fruity pulp. One by one, I separated the seeds from the pulp. Amazed by the abundant harvest, I stacked the ka`kao seeds in a pyramid on the ground.

So proud of my accomplishment, I selected two of the harvested seeds. I held one seed in each hand and reached out to show Ka`Kao.

"What do you want?" she asked.

I stared at the tree, unsure what she meant.

Ka`Kao spoke again, her voice light and inquisitive. "What do you really want?"

"What do I want?" I repeated the question, stalling for time. No one had ever asked me this question before. I fidgeted nervously, not sure how to answer. I was afraid I'd get it all wrong.

"Your wants awaken your passions," said Ka`Kao. "Your passions lead you to your dreams. Your dreams hold the remembering of what you love about life. Feel your aliveness. Feel the callings of your heart."

But what if my dreams were too big, too far out of reach? What if my dreams didn't mean very much? What if no one else wanted what I wanted? What if nobody approved?

"What do you *really really really* want?" Ka`Kao's joyful voice called me out of the battle in my mind.

I reached toward the sky, holding a ka`kao seed in my open hand. "I want the tree frogs to sing," I declared, hoping the entire rainforest could hear.

I held up the other ka`kao seed. "I *really really*

really want to be me," I called to the treetops. "I want to feel happy. I want to be free." It was liberating speaking the words out loud. I felt exhilarated sharing my dreams.

"Place the seeds carrying your dreams down into the soils of the earth," said Ka`Kao.

I put both seeds in the hole I'd dug near Ka`Kao's roots. I covered the seeds with a layer of flower petals, cherishing the simple beauty of my garden of dreams. Looking back to Ka`Kao, I asked, "Now what?"

"More dreams," she said.

"More dreams?" I was taken by surprise. "With all of these?" The pyramid of harvested seeds suddenly looked daunting.

"Set aside the worries," said Ka`Kao. "Reach past the fears. Dream a new dream with each and every seed."

I stayed up all night dreaming more dreams. At first, I spoke hesitantly about what I really wanted. I had to muster up the courage. I fumbled to find the words. It didn't take long, though, before I felt fully inspired. I was surprised to discover how many dreams I had for my life, for the rainforest, for the earth, for all life. I loved picturing the world I wanted to live in and leave behind for my children, for my children's children, for all the generations to come. I spoke from my heart, more honest than I'd ever been.

When the sky brightened with the morning light, I held the last seed and dreamed one more dream. Scooping up handfuls of blossoms, leaves, and dirt, I buried the dreamseeds near the roots of Ka`Kao.

Tired and content, I leaned back against the tree trunk. The last thing I saw before I fell asleep was the emerald frog hopping around on the pillowy heap of buried dreamseeds, packing it down for safekeeping.

Crystal Tapestry

In the steamy afternoon heat, I was shaken awake by rumbling thunder, flashes of lightning, and pouring rain. I could see the emerald frog sitting on the mound of dreamseeds. I felt soothed by the frog's tranquility. He was steadily anchored in the midst of the storm.

"What do I do now?" I asked Ka'Kao Tree.

"Every seed carries vast fields of knowledge—about who the seed will become, about what will nourish growth, about the web of relationships needed to flourish and thrive. Seeds hold the blueprint for life," said Ka'Kao. "Your dreams are a universe of knowledge too. They carry the remembering of what you love about life. Your dreams hold the blueprint for what is readying to grow. Honor your dreams. Feed your dreams. Surround the dreamseeds with loving care while they're held here in the fertile soils of the earth."

Day after day, I spent hours sitting by Ka'Kao's roots and tending to the dreamseeds. I loved revisiting the dreams that I'd dreamed, holding the pictures in my mind. Sometimes the feelings were so vivid and clear, I felt my dreams were already alive.

The more time I spent with Ka'Kao Tree, the more I could see the wide-open circle of relationships she had. Birds, frogs, and lizards rested in Ka`Kao's branches. The blossoms and leaves that fell to the ground fertilized the soil. Rains came, feeding Ka`Kao's roots. Tiny insects pollinated her blossoms. The canopy high overhead provided shade from the blazing tropical sun. Bats, parrots, and monkeys feasted on the fruit pods and dispersed the seeds on the ground, planting the next generation of trees. Ka`Kao was part of a never-ending dance of giving and receiving. I wanted to live like that too.

One night, as the light of the full moon trickled through the branches, I could see the tiny frog hopping excitedly overhead. I heard a muffled thud near the tree roots. The emerald frog leapt from Ka`Kao's branches and landed on top of the heavy object that had fallen to the ground. Curious, I leaned in closer. I couldn't believe my eyes.

I felt the sticky grip of the frog's tiny feet as he hopped up my arm. He perched on my shoulder, watching me examine the crystal we'd just found. The sparkling gemstone seemed to have fallen from the sky.

I lifted the crystal up into a sliver of moonlight. The glistening stone was beautiful beyond words. I felt the temptation to keep it, to claim it as my own. But in my heart of hearts, I sensed the crystal wanted to be returned home.

With my bare hands, I dug a hole beside the mound of dreamseeds. I buried the crystal in the soil near Ka`Kao's roots.

Ka`Kao Tree was watching over as Thea discovered the crystal. This sacred stone had been buried for many generations near the Old Woman's fire. Carried to the center of the rainforest by Jaguar, the crystal had been tucked away in Ka`Kao's branches. Touched by the moonlight and the emerald frog's tiny feet, the crystal had now found it's way into Thea's hands.

The crystal held the ancient promise of the turning of the times on the earth. Even if just one person remembered heart-centered ways of living, a powerful river of change would begin to flow.

Ka`Kao Tree sensed the shift as Thea returned the crystal to the land. This simple loving act had ripple effects far beyond what Thea could see.

Your Heart Is Your Guide

"**E**verything is ready now," Ka`Kao announced, waking me early one morning.

"Everything is ready?" I asked, sleepily stretching my arms toward the sky. "Ready for what?"

"Ready for your journey back to the river," she said.

A wave of worries rushed through my mind. I wanted to protest against Ka`Kao's unexpected announcement, but I couldn't organize my thoughts.

"Gather up the seeds you buried, the seeds that are carrying your dreams," Ka`Kao said. "Take them to the Old Woman by the River, the Keeper of the Fire." I recalled my prior meeting with the old woman. I had to admit she'd reached out kindly to me, giving me something to drink and letting me sit by the fire. But then she'd abruptly sent me away. Truth is she scared me. Not to mention the jaguar who was prowling around.

"I don't know the way back," I told Ka`Kao, hoping this excuse would convince her to let me stay.

"The Old Woman lives in the place where the land and the waters meet," said Ka`Kao. "You'll find your way."

"How?" I asked, on the verge of tears.

"Let your heart be your guide," said the tree.

I paced back and forth by the roots of Ka`Kao, longing for further instructions, hoping for some comforting words. But nothing more was said by the tree.

Reluctantly, I prepared for my journey. I dug up the seeds and carefully piled them in a hollow ka`kao pod. The natural beauty of the seeds evoked memories of my dreams, soothing my sadness and spurring me on to do what I needed to do. I wrapped a vine around the pod to hold the dreamseeds in place. I filled in the hole I'd dug and patted down the earth near Ka`Kao's roots, returning the land to the way it was before I came.

Looking around for the tree frog, I was disappointed I couldn't find him. Muttering a shy good-bye to the tree, I turned away. Stumbling through the mud, I got tangled in thorns and tripped over rocks. I couldn't figure out which way to go. I looked over my shoulder, glancing back toward Ka`Kao. It was hard to ignore the gnawing sensation that I'd left something unsaid and undone.

Walking back toward the tree, I plucked a red flower dangling from a vine. I stood beside Ka`Kao with the blossom in one hand, the dreamseed bundle in the other. I set the passionflower on the ground by Ka`Kao's roots. I thanked her for the gifts she'd given to me, the safe haven and guidance, her friendship and loving care.

I walked around the tree, taking one last look at the curved trunk and delicate branches, the smooth bark and broad green leaves. I admired the beauty of the plump, colorful pods. I leaned in close to the clusters of tiny blossoms, still curious why these flowers didn't have a fragrance I could detect. Soaking in the details, I sculpted an image of the tree in my mind. I wanted to remember her always.

I turned and headed on into the rainforest, determined now to find my way back to the Old Woman in the place where the land and the waters meet.

As Thea walked away, the red-eyed tree frog crawled down Ka`Kao's trunk. He leapt toward Thea and landed on the dreamseed bundle held in her hand. So small and light, the stowaway frog wasn't noticed. He scurried under the vine wrapped around the bundle and hid inside among the seeds.

10

Wind and Fire

Ka`Kao Tree called to the winds to blow blossoms from her branches and carry them all the way to the Old Woman by the River, the Keeper of the Fire.

Sparks flew as the shower of ka`kao blossoms fell into the flames. The Old Woman listened to the messages sent to her on the winds.

She dropped a golden nugget of tree resin onto a smoldering coal. A sweet fragrance drifted into the air, calling to the Old Woman's friend. Jaguar leapt from the trees with powerful grace. He landed without a sound beside the Old Woman. His eyes glowed brightly, reflecting the flickering light of the fire.

The Old Woman and the wildcat warmly greeted each other. "There's more for us to do," the Old Woman said. She held in her mind's eye a picture of Thea finding her way back from the center of the rainforest. "She's carrying a sacred dreamseed bundle. Walk close beside her. Protecting. Watching over. Unseen."

Jaguar pranced around the fire and soared over the flames, disappearing into the trees.

11

Guardian at the Gateway

Through thundering storms and stifling heat, I continued on through the rainforest. Whenever my determination wavered, I focused on my dreams. I reminded myself of Ka`Kao's certainty that I could find my way back to the Old Woman by the River. To brighten my spirit when my sense of adventure started to fade, I splashed around in the puddles and got covered with mud. That's when I caught a glimpse of the spotted tail of a giant snake.

Instinctively, I stepped away slowly and climbed on top of a moss-covered log. I was hoping not to be noticed. I respected the snake's existence and wanted to give her plenty of room to be who she was and do whatever she was here to do. I wanted to give myself the same respect too.

Standing on the fallen log, I had a bird's-eye view. I marveled at the graceful way the snake slithered through the mud. I was curious where she was going. Though I tried to be still and not make a sound until the snake was out of sight, I couldn't keep my balance on the slippery bark and decaying wood.

Anaconda swung her head around, honing in on my movement. Meeting eye to eye, we sized each other up. Mustering every ounce of courage,

I stepped to the ground and planted my feet on the muddy earth.

"I'm on my way back to the Old Woman by the River," I told the great serpent. I paused and took a breath, settling the quiver in my throat. "I'm bringing the Old Woman the seeds of Ka`Kao."

I placed the dreamseed bundle on the ground for Anaconda to see. I wanted her to know my words were trustworthy. I wanted to show her my intentions were sincere.

Anaconda slithered toward the bundle, brushing by Thea's feet. The serpent's forked tongue darted back and forth, touching the hollow ka`kao pod, examining the dreamseeds.

Anaconda detected the tiny frog crouched inside the pod. The serpent leaned in to investigate this surprising discovery. The emerald frog tucked himself deeper into the bundle of seeds, letting the serpent know he did not want his presence revealed.

Anaconda sensed the friendship between Thea

and the tree frog. The beauty of the dreams in the seed bundle was palpable. Thea was persevering, staying true to her heart. The Old Woman by the River would be pleased.

Anaconda returned her fiery gaze to Thea. The serpent nodded her massive head, pointing the way to a path hidden behind a cluster of blue flowers. Anaconda slithered away, dissolving into the wild tangle of vines.

12

Belongs with You

Thanking the anaconda, I picked up the dreamseed bundle. I crept through the thicket of blue flowers and found my way, step by step, along the mossy path. Thorns tugged at my hair and scratched my arms and legs. The sounds of the river currents grew louder, assuring me I was getting closer, guiding me through the path. I slid down the steep riverbank and splashed into the crystal clear water. Floating on my back, I watched the sunlight dance on the rippling water. I was thrilled to have made it this far.

After resting awhile, I waded to the riverbank and picked up the dreamseed bundle. Looking upstream and downstream, I found myself standing at a crossroads. I wasn't sure which way to go.

A luscious fragrance carried by the breeze wove its way into my awareness. Memories of the Old Woman, the roasting spices, and chocolatey drink instantly came alive. I ran along the riverbank, following the trail of the alluring scent.

Soon, though, my tiredness weighted me down. My feet dragged through the mud. I lost the trail of the scent. Doubts rattled around in my mind. I climbed to the top of a boulder, hoping to get my bearings. Maybe I'd see a familiar landmark.

Maybe I'd catch a glimpse of the smoke from the Old Woman's fire.

A menacing growl sent a chill up my spine. I slowly turned around, terrified to see who was there. Piercing gold eyes glared at me. The jaguar crouched low to the ground, ready to pounce.

My stomach lurched and I tumbled backward, falling off the boulder. Lying on the riverbank, I was certain I'd just fallen to my death. The jaguar approached and leaned in close, whiskers twitching, a deep guttural growl rumbling in his throat.

Face-to-face with the jaguar, the majestic beauty of the wildcat was all I could see. A flash of recognition passed between us. The jaguar darted away and leapt into the underbrush, vanishing into the rainforest.

I scrambled to my feet and stumbled a few clumsy steps. I froze in my tracks when I saw something moving along the riverbank. I stood still just long enough to see that it wasn't the wildcat coming back to finish the hunt.

The Old Woman walked toward me as if emerging out of a mirage. She was absolutely the most beautiful sight I'd ever seen. She dipped a gourd bowl into the river and reached out to me, offering a drink. The crystal clear water washed away my fears.

Not a word was spoken between us, though I understood I was to follow the Old Woman. I retrieved the dreamseed bundle from the riverbank where it'd fallen from my hands. I checked to make sure the ka'kao pod wasn't broken. The vine wrapping was still holding the dreamseeds in place.

I walked with the Old Woman to the forest clearing. Like the first night we'd met, we sat together by the fire. I watched the Old Woman toss twigs and leaves onto the coals, igniting orange and yellow flames. She moved with ease, like a dancer, in rhythm with the crackling fire.

The Old Woman was unlike anyone I'd ever met. What was she doing out here in the middle of nowhere? I wondered what she thought of me showing up again so unexpectedly in her world.

"Ka'Kao Tree sent me here," I explained. "I brought this for you." I handed her the dreamseed bundle. I sensed a deep well of love in the Old Woman as she cradled the ka`kao bundle in her hands. She looked closely at the dreamseeds tied with a passionflower vine.

"Hold onto your dreams," the Old Woman said. "Don't give them up. Don't give them away." She handed me the dreamseed bundle. "This belongs with you."

13

In the Circle

I was awakened by the enchanting sounds of the Old Woman singing. I slowly coaxed myself out of my resting place, curious how long I'd been asleep.

The sight of the jaguar circling around the fire shook me wide-eyed awake. I stared at the Old Woman, wordlessly pleading for help. Her peaceful, grounded stance let me know there was nothing to fear.

"Jaguar has been with you," the Old Woman said. "He's been walking close beside you. Making sure of your safe return."

With powerful feline grace, the wildcat leapt into a tree. He leisurely stretched out in the crook of a branch. I leaned back against the tree trunk, surprised by what I'd just learned. I hadn't really been alone. I'd been protected every step of the way. But how did the wildcat and the Old Woman know I was coming back?

I watched the Old Woman tending the fire. I listened to the soft swishing of Jaguar's tail. The relationship between the wildcat and the Old Woman was such a mystery. Their friendship bridged great differences. Their communication was made up of much more than words. Even though I was a stranger from a faraway place, they welcomed me in and offered companionship and care.

"Spread all the dreamseeds out in the sun," the Old Woman said. Her arms motioned like a gentle breeze, guiding the way toward a circle of stones. I walked around the circle, admiring the diverse stones nestled precisely together in a perfectly round ring.

Holding the dreamseed bundle, I sat on the ground in the center of the stone circle. I untied the passionflower vine wrapped around the ka`kao pod. The heaping pile of seeds, once carefully stacked, avalanched to the ground. A flash of emerald green caught my attention.

I saw a tiny tree frog hop out of the dreamseed bundle, leap across the ground, and land on top of a speckled stone. My surprise turned to delight when I recognized my friend. The tree frog had been with me on my journey back from the center of the rainforest, just like the wildcat had been.

I sat quietly awhile, marveling at the beauty of everyone around me—the Old Woman, the jaguar, the red-eyed tree frog, this magical place they called home. Their lives were woven together—no, wait.

I stopped to make a correction, even though I was only talking to myself.

Our lives were woven together—the Old Woman, the river, the fire, the wildcat, the tree frog, the dreamseeds, the circle of stones, and me. Fibers of connection were woven between us like a huge spider web, joining our lives, joining us with many others, the web spiraling far beyond what my eyes could see.

My delight was quickly overshadowed by confusion and guilt. How could I be happy when there still was so much more to do? I looked to the Old Woman, searching her eyes for answers. "The tree frogs aren't singing," I told her. The moment the words came out of my mouth, I had the feeling this was something she already knew.

"When tree frogs sing, they fill the rainforest with their colorful voices, with the very breath of life," the Old Woman said. "The trees breathe this in, soaking up the sharing. Then the trees breathe out sending waves of the breath of life rippling through the rainforest and far beyond."

With a smooth round rock, the Old Woman

pushed a lump of coal out of the fire and into a clay bowl. She dropped chunks of dried roots onto the glowing ember. The fragrant smoke hovered between us as the Old Woman walked around the circle of stones. "When tree frogs sing, they feed the rainforest," she said, her words in rhythm with her steps. "The breath of the rainforest feeds the Mother Earth. Filling the world with harmony. Weaving the web of life with love. When the web of life flourishes, the tree frogs flourish too. So the cycle continues, circling around and around. Songs being shared. Harmony being woven. Life being nourished. Day by day. Night after night.

"You can be a weaver of harmony too," the Old Woman said. She waved a brilliant green feather over the smoldering herbs. The fragrant smoke drifted toward the center of the stone circle where I sat with the dreamseed bundle. I breathed in deeply and a soothing sensation washed over me.

"Spread the dreamseeds out in the sun," the Old Woman said. One by one, I placed the brown seeds in a single layer on the ground. My memories carried me back to my time with Ka`Kao Tree, the joy of our friendship, the sense of peace and belonging I'd found. I was surprised, again, to see how many dreams I'd dreamed for my life, for the tree frogs, for the earth, for all life. The whole stone circle was filled.

The Old Woman taught me how to tend to the ka`kao seeds in her traditional ways. She explained that every seed needed plenty of time touching the earth and facing the sun. "The medicine in ka`kao deepens when the seeds are dried in the sun. Your dreams will be seasoning too," the Old Woman said. She described how the ka`kao seeds had to be turned over, again and again. "For many days," she told me. At first, this responsibility sounded tedious yet after a while became a cherished task.

The emerald frog showed up each evening for my turning of the seeds ceremony. I offered my gratitude and spoke about my dreams. The tiny red-eyed tree frog hopped from dreamseed to dreamseed, making sure I didn't miss a single one.

14

Tracks in the Sand

One afternoon, walking along the riverbank, I spotted a jaguar track. I knelt down and placed my hand beside the massive paw print. I respected

Jaguar's wildness and admired his protective spirit. I'd grown to love rather than fear the wildcat.

Following the trail of prints, I explored how it felt to walk in the way of the jaguar. My pace slowed. My focus deepened. My senses came alive. My body filled with the pure passion of the hunt.

Exhilarated, I came around the bend in the river. What I saw made my heart jump. The curved pieces of wood were barely visible in the dense underbrush. I reached out to touch the weathered wooden beams. This was the hull of my raft.

I was flooded with memories of getting stranded in the storm. I remembered that first startling glimpse of the Old Woman and Jaguar by the fire. But now, what was shaking my world upside down, was the realization that I could go home.

I spent the rest of the day cleaning up the raft. Leaves and twigs had piled up inside, blown in by the winds and saturated by rain. I removed the spiders who had taken up residence and brushed away their sticky webs.

I stood ankle-deep in the river currents, holding

tightly onto the raft so it didn't slip away. I checked for leaks and was thrilled to find the raft still could float. I splashed around in the crystal clear waters, celebrating. I could go home.

When the sunset colored the sky with streaks of orange and red, I pushed the raft underneath the overhanging tree branches. I observed the surroundings, making a mental map of the landmarks so I could find the location again.

As I walked back toward the fire, questions streamed through my mind. Should I tell the Old Woman about the raft? How much longer should I stay? How was I going to explain that I'd be leaving? We'd never spoken about this possibility before.

15

With Every Breath and Every Step

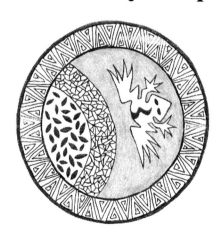

That evening, after my turning of the seeds ceremony, I sat with the Old Woman by the fire.

Despite the beautiful surroundings, our friendship, and the nourishing food, I felt uneasy. I hadn't said anything about finding my raft. I was afraid to talk about leaving. I pretended that nothing out of the ordinary had happened. I glanced sideways at the Old Woman, trying to figure out if she could tell I was hiding.

"Fears just muddy the waters," the Old Woman said as she gazed into the fire. "Dream Makers bring their dreams alive with every breath and every step they take."

Late in the night, I was jolted out of a fitful sleep. I sat up, determined to find the cause of the disturbance. The soft glow of the waning moon lit up the stone circle. The Old Woman was tending her fire. The emerald frog was perched on the speckled stone, as always, watching over the dreamseeds. Nobody else seemed troubled. Nothing looked out of place.

I lay back down, gruffly pushing around the cushion of leaves. I tossed and turned, growing more irritated with every passing minute. I couldn't get comfortable. It was impossible to get back to sleep. Finally I had to admit there was nobody to blame because the disturbance was coming from inside of me.

I wasn't being truthful. I was undermining my friendship with the Old Woman. I was sabotaging my own dreams.

I took a deep breath and walked toward the fire. The tiny emerald frog hopped along every step of the way. When the Old Woman looked at me, I felt warmth radiating from her eyes. She waited quietly until I was ready to speak.

"I found my way home," I said, my eyes brimming with tears. It was a bittersweet moment, a swirl of emotions—my love for the Old Woman, my sadness about leaving, the beauty of staying true to my heart. The Old Woman rustled through a basket and pulled out a colorful woven bundle. She unfolded the cloth wrappings and held out a heaping pile of dark chocolates.

I'd watched her make these tempting treats. It was a meticulous, ceremonial affair. After grinding roasted ka`kao seeds into a velvety paste, she'd sprinkled in spices and added a few drops of honey. The chocolatey concoction was then shaped into small mounds. The arrangement of luscious dark chocolates on layers of leaves looked like a constellation of stars. Later, the Old Woman gathered up the chocolates, wrapped them in cloth bundles, and stored them in her baskets. I had been waiting and hoping, ever since, to have a taste.

"Thank you," I said, thoroughly delighted. I selected one of the handcrafted delicacies made from the seeds of Ka`Kao. Trying to be polite, I took a little nibble. The spicy chocolate was so delicious I quickly devoured the rest. The Old Woman reached out with the bundle of chocolates, generously offering more.

Drink in Your Dreams

I spent the next several days gathering supplies and stocking the raft. I was excited about the adventure ahead. Yet still, it was hard to think about saying good-bye.

One evening, during my ceremonial turning of the seeds, the Old Woman walked over from her fire. I sensed her keen attention focused directly on me. I could feel her close examination of the dreamseeds.

"Everything is ready," she said, looking deeply into my eyes.

"Ready for what?" I asked.

"Ready for the making," she explained.

The Old Woman placed a large wooden bowl on the ground. "Collect the seeds," she said, "and bring them to the fire."

With the tree frog watching over, I gathered the dreamseeds. I dropped them, one by one, into the wooden bowl, envisioning each and every dream. I walked to the Old Woman's fire, holding the bowl close to my body. I was careful not to drop any of the seeds. I didn't want to leave behind any dreams.

The Old Woman set the dreamseeds on a large, flat rock that was nestled in the hot, glowing coals. As the seeds roasted over the fire, the outer shell thinned and hardened. When the roasted seeds were cool enough to touch, the Old Woman selected one seed. She broke apart the hardened outer shell. She piled the shredded pieces of shell onto a stone, and dropped the winnowed ka`kao seed into a gourd bowl.

"The shell has been protecting the life of the seed," the Old Woman said. "The shell has served it's purpose and is no longer needed now." She brushed the wispy, broken bits off the stone and into the fire. The flames crackled, quickly burning the shell away.

With a nudging look in her eyes, the Old Woman let me know the rest was up to me. Dreamseed by dreamseed, I separated the seeds from the outer shells. I set the shredded shells on the stone and piled the winnowed seeds in the bowl. The dreamseeds felt smooth and looked even darker brown, as if they'd been polished.

"Give to the fire what is no longer needed," said the Old Woman.

I brushed the pile of shredded shells into the flames. As I watched the sparks fly, I asked the spirit of the fire to help clear away anything blocking my heart. I blew on the feathery bits still stuck on my hands. I asked the spirit of the fire to help me let go of any lingering judgments and doubts. The shells floated on the air, fell into the flames, and quickly turned to ash.

The Old Woman began grinding the dreamseeds between two heavy rocks. When she spoke, the rhythm of her voice sounded like an ancient chant.

"These are the sacred seeds from Ka`Kao. They carry her medicine and are infused with your dreams," the Old Woman said. "They've been nourished in the fertile soils of the earth, watched over by the tree frog, and honored by Anaconda. The dreamseeds have soaked in the sun. They've been saturated with the light of the moon and the stars. The seeds and your dreams have been brushed by the winds, touched by the rains, and warmed by the fire."

The Old Woman ground the seeds until they transformed into a dark, velvety paste. "Jaguar has been protecting the Dream Maker," she said, a glint in her mahogany eyes. "The dreamseeds have been cared for by you and me. There's a weaving of harmony. Here, have a taste."

I dipped my finger into the rich, creamy ka`kao. The pure essence of the fire-roasted stoneground seeds burst alive in my mouth. The Old Woman poured the velvety paste into a pot, blending the ka`kao with crystal clear river water. I rustled around in the woven baskets, searching for the ingredients the Old Woman requested. I handed her pinches of red and gold powders, and bits of cinnamon bark and vanilla bean. As she sprinkled these into the cooking pot, a colorful trail of spices spiraled into the chocolatey mixture.

While the dreamseed elixir warmed over the fire, an irresistible fragrance floated by. Every now and then, the Old Woman stirred the brew and added another pinch or two of spices. I watched and waited until the Old Woman determined it was time.

She poured the ka`kao elixir into a gourd cup, filling it to the brim. "Drink in your dreams," she said. Sip by sip, I relished every delicious drop. The Old Woman refilled my cup.

Although this was a night of celebration, I felt keenly aware of the pending good-byes. I gazed into the fire, savoring my dreamseed elixir, pondering the mysteries of life. I decided I could embrace all of it. I could be accepting of every little bit. The endings. The beginnings. The in-betweens. All of life. Everyone. All of me.

Homecoming

Late in the night, I fell asleep in the stone circle on the ground where the dreamseeds had been. When I woke early the next morning, the emerald tree frog was sitting nearby on his favorite speckled stone. I realized now that it wasn't only the dreamseeds he'd been watching over ever since we'd met.

When the sky brightened with the sunrise, the Old Woman walked over from her fire. She set a bowl of smoldering herbs outside the stone circle. A peaceful sensation flowed through me as I breathed in the fragrant smoke. I sensed the Old Woman knew what I knew. The time had come for us to say good-bye.

"The stone circle is ready to be taken apart," she said, kindness emanating from her eyes. The Old Woman described her traditional ways for taking down the stone altar. I walked around the circle, feeling gratitude with every step, picking up the stones one by one. I gave thanks to the land and all the beings, seen and unseen, who had created sacred space for the dreamseeds and me.

The last stone I picked up was the tree frog's favorite. I tucked the speckled stone in my pocket as a keepsake. I wanted the tree frogs to know I'd heard their silence. I was listening to their call to the people of the earth, to me, to us, to bring the ways of harmony back.

I scattered the rest of the stones behind the tangle of vines to honor the place I'd hidden that first night I'd shown up. This was sacred ground too, though I wouldn't have believed that back then. In the wisdom of her ways, with some kind of magic, the Old Woman had helped me keep walking in the direction of my dreams. She'd nourished me, nudged me, invited me to take a step, and then left it up for me to choose.

When I finished clearing away the stone circle altar, I walked to the fire and sat beside the Old Woman. I handed her the gift I'd made. She warmly received the ka`kao pod filled with bundles of her cherished herbs.

I could have talked for hours, telling the Old Woman how much she meant to me, how grateful I was that our paths had crossed, how sad I was to say good-bye. I could have blurted out the many questions I still had about her. I could have shared my hopes that we'd see each other again. But there really was no need for words. Sitting side by side by the crackling fire, we simply enjoyed the joy of being together.

Finally I stood up, walked to the riverbank, and headed downstream toward my raft. Before I rounded the bend in the river, I looked back one last time. The wildcat was stretched out leisurely on a tree branch. As always, the Old Woman was tending the fire.

18

When Tree Frogs Sing

I pulled the raft out from beneath the trees and double-checked my supplies. Everything was ready. There was no excuse not to leave, nothing to hold me back. As I pushed the raft across the muddy riverbank and into the water, I was surprised to see the red-eyed tree frog sitting on the wooden hull. His sticky-toed orange feet held him securely in place as the raft swayed in the currents. For a brief sweet moment, I thought he was coming with me. But he jumped away and disappeared into the rainforest.

I peered into the trees, hoping for one last glimpse of my friend. The tiny emerald tree frog was an unexpected teacher who'd shown me what he'd known all along. That harmony flows from the inside out. That our lives are interwoven, everyone here in the rainforest with everyone on the earth with everyone everywhere in the extraordinary web of life. That whatever you do, wherever you are, ripples out and touches life near and far.

I hopped into the raft and reached out over the hull, sprinkling a handful of red blossoms into the water. I was grateful the river had brought me here. I asked the river for help in finding my way home. I didn't have a specific destination in mind. "Let your heart be your guide," Ka'Kao Tree had told me. That's what I was going to do. I scattered another handful of blossoms in the river and watched the petals float downstream.

It was a long day traveling on the river. I got soaked by the rains and heated by the sun. I pushed the raft around logjams and sloshed through the mud. I rested in the shade under thick tangles of vines. Howler monkeys howled. Flocks of birds chattered. Swarms of buzzing bugs incessantly hummed. Blue butterflies fluttered by. Snakes slithered along the water's edge. I just kept going, no matter what I came across. It was a challenge but not a battle. It felt more like a dance.

At sunset, I pulled the raft on shore and set up my camp for the night. With great care, I lifted the lid of the clay bowl I'd been given. I peered inside and felt warmth on my face. The lumps of coal from the Old Woman's fire were still alive. I poured the glowing embers onto the ground and added leaves, twigs, and chunks of bark. The smoke thickened. The kindling sparked. Like magic, the fire blazed to life.

Sitting beside the fire, I unwrapped the cloth bundle. I'd been looking forward to this feast all day. "Food for the heart," the Old Woman had said when she'd handed me the bundle of delicious dark chocolates. Even though there were many miles between us, I could picture the light in the Old Woman's mahogany eyes.

Later that night, I heard rustling in the leaves. I stood up, my senses immediately awake and aware, tracking the source of the sound. In the flickering firelight, I noticed something moving in the trees. No, wait—I stopped to correct myself. It wasn't some thing. There were many some *ones*.

Countless tiny tree frogs were hopping through the branches and leaping from leaf to leaf. A high-pitched peep rang out from the treetops. Then I heard a chirp. Then another. More tree frogs joined in, sharing their colorful songs. A wild symphony burst alive.

Standing on the riverbank, I breathed in the beauty. The exuberant harmony rained down on the earth and floated along the river currents and drifted through the rainforest canopy.

JoAnne Dodgson

www.joannedodgson.com

CPSIA information can be obtained
at www.ICGtesting.com
Printed in the USA
FFOW02n0933281217
44282043-43843FF